CW00920119

CONTENTS

THE START....

CHAPTER 1

I don't have a lot of memories of my childhood. I do however remember staying at my grandparents a lot. I would stay at my dad's parents on a Friday and then I would go up to my mum's parents on a Saturday. For years I lived in complete ignorance as to why I would spend a lot of time with my grandparents but when I look back now it was probably to shield me from the abuse that enshrouded our family's life and to protect me from any harm. I would spend time with my cousins during these trips and loved every moment of this, having fun, watching cartoons and playing outside.

When I was around six years old I was extremely sick with mumps, a condition that affects the throat. I remember feeling really ill and wanting to curl up in a heap on the couch. I specifically remember this time as it was the first time I felt like my dad was my dad, as opposed to some stranger who happened to live in our house. Sadly I don't have many memories of my dad being a good father, bar this one time.

This sick day was probably one of the only days I wasn't outside exploring the beauty of a spherical object (a football!) by kicking it against a wall. My dad came in from work at around tea-time and he brought with him the distinctive aroma that he brought home every evening, wood dust mixed with stale beer and cigarettes. That night was different though as it was the night that my dad brought me home football stickers! I'd never had any of them before and it was as if all my dreams had come true! In my first packet of six Scottish football stickers I got two players from Glasgow Rangers and another few that I don't recall. That didn't matter though as I had found the team that I would support and my dad had helped me do that! Even though he was a Hearts fan and thought they were the best team in the world, I was grateful for my father's help in finding my football team.

My parents were from two different backgrounds. My dad was brought up in a Roman Catholic family and my mum was from a Protestant upbringing, both of which were not practised in either of their lives at this time. My mum was born in Glasgow and brought up near Bridgeton Cross on Baltic Street. At a very young age she moved to an area 24 miles east along the M8 motorway to a town named Whitburn in West Lothian in what was called the Glasgow overspill. (This was an initiative set up to ease the ever-growing city of Glasgow by encouraging families to move to smaller towns.) Daughter to Billy and Fay and sister to William and Stephen, my mum left school and worked in a shop in a town called Armadale, where she later met my father. My dad was born and grew up in that same town in West Lothian. He was son to John and Catherine and brother to Samuel, Jean, David (who passed away in 2007) and John jr.

My parents were married in 1976 and I reckon I was at the wedding as I was conceived just before. They moved into my childhood family home in Armadale. This was to be the stage for my earliest memory. I would later learn when my father passed away in 2016 that he had in fact started going back to Catholic mass as he wanted desperately to abstain from alcohol as this had robbed him of his health. At his funeral I learnt that the altar the priest was speaking from in the chapel was in fact built by my dad who was known in his home town as a master joiner. (I clearly have not inherited this though as my skill set certainly does not include DIY!) I recall my dad building things in the house such as the breakfast bar and cupboards. Whenever I smell woodwork it evokes strong emotions as it takes me back to times in my early childhood.

CHAPTER 2

My fascination for football went from collecting stickers to kicking a football around the local park with my friends, I loved playing it. During the summer I'd put my football shoes on in the morning as soon as I was ready to go out and wouldn't stop kicking a ball till my mum shouted me back in when dusk started to fall. It was around this time that life at home became a little busier. I was eight when I found out that there was to be an extra addition to our household. When Steven was born in July 1984 my mum stayed in the hospital to have surgery. My new-born brother was sent off to our grandparents home three miles away and so I didn't get to see him for the first three weeks of his life. This separation was set to continue as my later addiction to prescription drugs and alcohol would rob my brother and I of most of our childhood years. I do remember fondly, taking my little brother out in his buggy for walks to the nearby park that wasn't that far away from our house. I ran at great speed around a dirt bike track with Steven in his little buggy loving every minute of our adventure! Sadly these are the few good memories I have from my childhood, as close to my thirteenth birthday my life and the life of my family changed drastically.

My childhood was spent between two towns in central Scotland, 'Armadale' the town that I grew up in until the age of 13, and 'Whitburn', the town which I moved to after my parents' separation and eventual divorce. Both these towns at that time had a population of around 11,000 people living in them. All through my primary school education I attended Armadale primary which was a positive time in my life as it brought about new challenges. I found it quite difficult to make friends so attending school forced me to try harder. I also wasn't great at listening to the teacher's instructions which often resulted in me receiving a barrage of warnings about how I would get nowhere in life if I couldn't listen in class! I did make friends though (even if I didn't lis-ten) which at the time was the greater of the two, as my parent's complicated relationship at home made time out of school very difficult.

At the age of twelve I attended karate lessons for over a year and became quite the student... At last, I had found an activity that kept my attention span for more than a few minutes! The teachers at the club, Stevie and Drew, were two of the most disciplined men I had ever met and I was drawn to them as they were real positive influences in my life at that time. The lessons were midweek and I rarely missed one, however, as I mentioned earlier, close to my thirteenth birthday all was about to change.

GROWING UP TOO QUICKLY......

CHAPTER 3

It probably started when I was really young. Late at night I'd hear muffled, raised voices followed by the sound of loud crashes. Then terrified female sobbing. My dad was an abusive man though never violent to me or my brother. In the dead of night he would regularly attack my mother who was blinded by her love for him. My dad was an alcoholic and drank as a means to get through the day. When I was turning thirteen he was drinking most days and didn't see the damage that alcohol was doing to him physically and emotionally. Close to my birthday Steven and I were in our room and after promising Steven for what felt like the thousandth time that mum was alright and it was just an argument, something in me told me to go downstairs and sort it out. It took me what seemed an eternity to walk down the short flight of stairs. When I finally gained the courage to walk through the door I was greeted by the sarcastic tone of a drunken abuser and a whimpering woman hiding her face. I cracked. I don't recall the actual events but it resulted in my mum and us boys leaving the next day and going to my grandparents to live.

Mum told us that she'd left a letter stating that we were gone and would not be returning. My Dad later told us that this letter broke his heart and that he cried for weeks. At the time I didn't believe a word that he said however when I look back I wonder if he maybe did feel devastated. Domestic abuse comes in many forms and affects so many individuals, from the victim to the perpetrator and all those in-between. When I think back I never feared that I would be hurt, but I feared for others. Whenever I heard arguing or shouting it filled me with immense anxiety and a real sense that I could not control these events. Whenever I now see aggression or injustice I get a sense that I should do something and I reckon this stems from the times when I felt helpless as a child. It fills me with great sadness that I ignored my dad for years after this and never challenged him on why he was acting this way. Choosing to ignore him only fuelled my hatred for him. Maybe if I'd confronted the issues during my adult years, I may have gained some understanding.

They say that your schooldays are the best days of your life. I can't recall this being a reality during my secondary education, as I soon became so desperate to leave that I developed a habit of not going! This had its repercussions! The truancy officer arrived at our door enquiring why I was not in the class that my mum thought I was in! This soon became a regular occurrence in my third year at school. When I wasn't in school I felt so free; there were no controlling teachers boring me to tears with what I perceived as their total draconian ideals. I was free to explore the outside world with all its glory, never thinking about the missed opportunities of my education.

I had started smoking when I was twelve years old and it was around this time that I first sniffed solvents. I don't recall liking them but I did it anyway just purely for the buzz. Drinking and taking recreational drugs I loved; I first smoked cannabis when I was fourteen years old and hung around the local park with a gang known as the CPP (Corrie Park Posse). We would regularly meet in the park to sniff solvents and kick a ball about before going to pick a fight with other gangs. After taking a few puffs on the joint I felt so relaxed and excited - at last I'd tried what everyone was talking about! The problem was, when I smoked and drank at the same time it gave me the foolish confidence of five men. I'd brazenly chat to girls and jump into any situation that arose at the flick of a switch. Of course this only led to trouble. I had been in fights before but none on the scale of what took place in the local park after an evening of cider and drugs. It started out as a joke but escalated with such ferocity that it took me by surprise. I started teasing a girl I used to go to school with. Her boyfriend who was a good few years older didn't take this too well and jumped me. With the concoction of drugs and alcohol in my system and also the fact he was twice the size of me, I got my first thumping. Thankfully it didn't last long as my cousin was in the park at the same time and jumped in to stop the onslaught of violence.

You'd think that after receiving a beating that I'd wise up and think about situations before jumping head first into them. This was not the case though as the next chance I got I was head first into situations without a care for the consequences. My immature peers didn't discourage me, and sadly, nor did the man who should've had the most influence in my life - my dad.

During this period in my life I travelled every weekend with my brother the three miles between my mums flat in Whitburn and my dad's house in Armadale. My dad had access to us every weekend and was obliged to make regular payments of maintenance to my mum as a result of a court case in which mum got full custody. Of course as a young boy I took advantage and would rip dad off at every opportunity. Looking back now I can see that this arrangement must have been difficult for my parents. It's often too easy to just buy a child's affection rather than give him/her the attention and love they really need.

When we moved I felt as if my world and everything in it had been turned upside down. Both my parents started seeing different people almost straight away and it wasn't long until the people they started seeing moved in. My earliest memories of the times when I had the joy of barging into their bedroom and jumping onto the bed and laughing were slowly fading away. Strangers had infiltrated our family circle and I was expected to respect them, a daunting task for a tearaway teenager.

CHAPTER 4

My mum and Robert (who she would eventually marry when I was around 18 years old) set up home in her flat in Whitburn with myself and Steven. I lived in an area of Whitburn called Blaeberry hill which was considered by some a non-desirable area to live in as the residents were mostly people who didn't work and were on social security. Whitburn had at one time been an industrial town with several different job opportunities including a coal mine and lots of industrious factories (including car manufacturers and a Levi Strauss clothes factory) however these were closed in the mid-1980s during the Thatcher years. Consequently the town, along with the surrounding towns, went into decline.

We lived in the third set of flats (which I've recently discovered have been demolished). Each evening after I had rushed my dinner down my throat as quick as it had been set down before me, I would head out. I'd ignore any homework that I had been assigned in favour of hanging around the local area and causing mischief. Smoking pot and sipping on my favourite tipple of a well-known tonic wine, became my daily routine.

Staying between parents' homes whilst growing up was extremely difficult as they tended to play us off against each other. This only annoyed me as a child as I hated to hear one parent disrespecting the other. Staying at dad's house was different from mum's as he seemed to care even less about what I got up to. We would spend time in the house drinking cider and he would also take me to his local bar to play pool where we would spend most of the evening drinking and chatting with all his friends. In his early years dad had been a successful amateur boxer who had a reputation of being a good fighter both inside and outside the ring. When he walked into a bar in town I got the impression that people genuinely wanted to talk to him or be in his company and definitely didn't want to offend him. As an impressionable teenager this made time with him all the more desirable.

In between spending time at my dad's and mum's houses I developed a love and a dependence on drugs. What had started off as a weekend pastime had now grown dangerously. I could regularly be found hanging around the blocks of flats that had become my haunt, smoking drugs and delving into the darker world of speed and ecstasy (amphetamine, uppers). I would also swallow copious amounts of diazepam and temazepam to make the pain of coming down from the uppers more bearable. Despite this terrible cycle, I had somehow managed to secure myself a job at a fruit and vegetable wholesalers.

CHAPTER 5

The business was owned by the Marshall brothers and they managed the company that delivered fruit and vegetables around the central belt area of Scotland, West Lothian and parts of Edinburgh. They also covered parts of South Lanarkshire and sometimes even into Glasgow. The lorry that I was "second man" in (the job entailed doing all the heavy work of carrying the produce into shops from the lorry) travelled through some of the roughest towns that I had ever seen. These were areas that were fine to go into during the day but were not so desirable at night.

Working at Marshall wasn't the most pleasurable or easiest of jobs, it was extremely hard work. Also, the verbal abuse that I would receive from the brothers who owned the business was difficult to take. They were proper old school employers; there was no union and indeed no rights as a worker. The job itself consisted of doing the odd night shift and also day shifts which started at 5am in the morning. Considering I was heavily into the drug "speed / amphetamine" and partying until three in the morning this proved almost impossible! The effects of speed are one of pure euphoria mixed with the deepest feelings of paranoia and anxiety that I have ever felt. It is such an addictive drug; I first used it when I did a night shift at Marshall's.

When I first took the drug I worked all night and when the morning time came I wondered where the night had gone! It was such a buzz, like nothing I'd ever had in my life. The next time I took it was at a party in Whitburn that took place every Thursday evening in a block of flats. It usually went on to Tuesday of the next week; people would stay over and continue partying when they awoke the next day, that's even if they slept.

I met a guy called Stuart who also worked at Marshalls. We quickly became best mates. We skipped school and hung around the shops drinking and generally making a nuisance of ourselves. One of our favourite pastimes was drinking a bottle of 'Buckfast'(cheap wine) between us as fast as we could – not at all mature! My behaviour at home was also poor as I was disrespectful towards my mum and step dad. I would stumble in the door at about 1am under the influence of something, waking the neighbours with my drunken antics. This went on for a while until my mother could take no more. At the age of sixteen I was thrown out of home.

I moved about half a mile up the road to my grandparents' home. This lasted around six months. I would go to work (I'd moved from the job at Marshalls to various different jobs including a slaughterhouse and also many different factory jobs) then would meet up with friends to get drunk or to use drugs. At such a young age I had ventured into a road of self-destruction which involved stealing to feed a habit. I would unashamedly dip my hand in my gran's pocket and steal her spare change and

I also would wait until my grandfather came home from the pub and fell asleep on the chair before grabbing the money that fell from his pocket. My poor grandfather had no clue that I was stealing his whisky and topping it up with water.

HOMELESS AT 17......

CHAPTER 6

Not surprisingly they also threw me out. This time it was for real; homeless at seventeen I had nowhere to go, no other lifeline and had burnt all my bridges. I had no Social Worker to bail me out or find me somewhere to go so I had to take responsibility for myself. I found a hostel which was in a town called Livingston. The hostel was named 'Open Door' and catered for young homeless people who were between the ages of 16-21. It didn't sink in at first. As a troubled teenager I hadn't really grasped the fact that this was in fact my own fault and so I blamed all the people around me. I wasn't ready to show any emotion about the hurt that was evident in my life; hurt that had been caused by my parents' separation; hurt that reminded me of my failure at school; hurt that was the result of rejection. I had wrongly tried to block these emotions out by drinking vast amounts of alcohol and using mind altering drugs. But the truth was, the hurt remained.

The hostel was in an area of Livingston known as Craigshill, a run-down area directly opposite a bar. I went there only once as it became clear very quickly that the locals didn't want any new faces around. I made a sharp exit and never returned. My memories of the hostel are good ones as there was always a hot meal ready for me and the milk was on tap... (In the kitchen that is...there was a milk vending machine in the kitchen.) On a weekend, there were opportunities to watch TV all day or watch videos to keep yourself entertained. The workers in the hostel were all very enthusiastic about their jobs and this showed in their relationships with the residents. They offered support 24hours a day and were there just in case anything kicked off.

I remember with fondness meeting a female member of staff who was assigned as my keyworker on several occasions to discuss my options for move on and what I could see myself doing in the future (Both of which are questions that you ask an adult and not a sixteen-year-old trying to be an adult?!) The woman was doing a job that I had no idea at the time that I would be doing myself later on in my life. Even when I was messing up, God was working out His plans!

I stayed in this hostel for about eight weeks and at the end of this short stay I had a successful move on to another hostel. It was in a nearby town called Bathgate and was a hostel for men and women of all ages. This was very eye opening for a teenager! The main difference in this hostel was that meals were not provided so I had to buy my own food and toiletries. Here I met one of the coolest guys that I had ever met. His name was Gary; he was English and had moved up to Scotland with his family. Their relationship had broken down and so he found himself homeless, like me. We quickly became friends as we had the same interests and also a common goal which was to get as drunk as we could and as quick as we could. We would get our money from the social security agency and we also had girlfriends who we heavily relied on to buy us alcohol so that we would not be without. We would take turns to buy cheap wine or whatever we could afford and would make an attempt to buy some groceries so that we had something to eat. Gary knew how to cook as he had been doing this for most of his life so he took the time to teach me how to cook up some basic meals. One of my favoured meals that he taught me to cook was Spaghetti Bolognese which was a cheap and easy meal to make. The rest of our money went on cigarettes. I only stayed at this hostel for a few months and spent most of this time partying with friends. In more recent years, I found Gary through social media and learnt that soon after this he went into the forces and spent the majority of his time in service. I was so relieved and immensely proud of the man that he turned out to be.

CHAPTER 7

Whilst living in these hostels I didn't work; I claimed money from the social security and quite liked the idea of getting money for nothing. However I had a desire to work and when my mother decided to give me another chance and take me back into her home, I commenced work back at the fruit and veg company. This time I was doing my driving lessons and envisioned myself driving before too long. Being a second man on a lorry delivering fruit and vegetables was tough physical work and long hours with very little pay. I worked for £11 a day and made more with working a bit of overtime. I also sold a small amount of drugs (Amphetamine) to make ends meet and remember selling gram wraps to a friend who was working ridiculously long hours as a security guard. He needed the drugs to keep him awake and I distinctly remember ripping him off as I would often only give him a half gram wrap and charge for a full gram. However, he kept coming back for his 'gram' and I continued to supply his needs.

Unfortunately, my eagerness to work at Marshall's didn't last long as the company had severe cash flow problems that they couldn't get out off so the company closed and as quick as I had got into a good paying job I was quickly out of it once more. This time it would not be as easy to pick myself up. My journey would now commence as a 'jobseeker' receiving money for sitting on my rear end doing nothing and tripping every fort-night to a town three miles walk away to sign on and lie incessantly through my teeth that I had been applying for job after job. I got used to the system very quickly and how to scam it. On any day I could be found at the dole office with some other lame excuse to try and ex-tract money that I should have been working for.

Being back at my mums didn't last very long and I even-tually moved on again. I moved in with my then girl-friend and her brother and his partner in a town called Boghall in a flat in a rough estate. At first this was an enjoyable experience as we would all meet up on Friday nights to party late into the weekend. My experience is really a blur as my time there was used up snorting amphetamine and smoking cannabis along with drink-ing alcohol. My love for amphetamine escalated to the level where I would visit my dealer every few days to get more drugs on 'tick' (buy now pay later). Using was an escapism from the real issues that I would not deal with until my mid-twenties.

My time in Boghall ended when I was involved in a fight with the friend I was living with and I was asked to leave the house and made street homeless again. My next move would be to return to Whitburn and present myself to the council offices to ask for assistance with finding accommodation. I knew that there was a vacant flat in a street that I was familiar with, a friend of mine had let me know that it had laid empty for months and was almost ready for move in. I was given the option to view this flat and after spending a few minutes I informed the housing officer that I would take it. In order to speed up the process I advised them that I would complete the maintenance issues myself. When I moved in I was helped out with furniture by family (My mum and my aunt furnished the flat with spare bits and pieces that they had lying around, my Gran paid for a couch and a bed.) Looking back now, it's amazing that they wanted to be bothered with me, but I'm so thankful that God had His hand upon me even when I was so far from Him.

The flat was in an area of Whitburn that I was familiar with, and it wasn't long until my friends knew that I had moved back to the area and it was turned into a drug den that would be used for parties for the next few years. The neighbours were older than me (in their 60s) and I quickly made a bad impression on them with my partying. Believe it or not, I did attempt to keep the place relatively tidy and tried to hold down several jobs, but my drug use had spiralled out of control. I was 20yrs old and living in the town that I had grown up in but I was suffering with depression and anxiety. On the outside I looked like I was a confident young man, on the inside I was slowly deteriorating as my mental health issues started to increase. I often would spend days in a darkened room only going outside to get some alcohol or some drugs to keep me going until I had the confidence to go out again. There were also occasions when I would attempt to stop using drugs and alcohol and I would cage myself up in my flat with all the lights out and start detoxing from substances. Sadly it never lasted, as I always had negative influences calling at my door. I remember walking home to my flat at times in utter fear for my life as my mind was filled with paranoid thoughts that people were going to attack me for no reason. I would make a fist and stick a key through my fingers and I was ready to stick this into the face of anyone who approached me. I was ready to defend myself even if that meant hurting someone else. This level of paranoia meant that I could not trust anyone. I felt the need to put up four or five sets of curtains on my window in my bedroom in order that no one would be able to see that I was in. The TV was turned down low, and I lived in paranoid distress.

CHAPTER 8

My experience with drugs took me to some weird and dangerous places and sometimes I look back and wonder how I ever survived. I remember a time when I went to another town in a car full of my friends. A contact had put a word in with a dealer to give us a few ounces of drugs on lay away. We ended up at her house which looked really respectable (She was a Granny and the house was filled with photos of her extended family.) and a far cry from the usual places that I frequented for drugs. I was in the house for approximately 10 minutes, got the drugs and had agreed a repayment date. I was about to leave when she appeared at the window of the car and tapped on the window with an actual sword in her hand. She shouted in my direction that if we didn't come back with the money on the agreed date that this was what we could expect. Needless to say this was a drug debt that I actually did pay.

I would love to say that my time using drugs and alcohol was so glamorous but this was far from true, in fact I was slowly deteriorating physically and mentally. My personal hygiene was non-existent and I rarely ate. I had long bouts of depression where I would not leave the house for days and wallow in self-pity. I was trapped in a vicious cycle of despair.

FROM NO HOPE TO FULL OF JOY.......

CHAPTER 9

My time in Whitburn was coming to an end as I was starting to get into debt with people who were dangerous and not the kind of people you wanted to owe money to. In the summer of 1998 I was walking home from a bar when I passed a massive sign on the wall that I had passed probably hundreds of times before and had taken no interest in. The sign was a scripture from the Bible and was from John 3:16: "For God so loved the world that he gave his only son that whosoever believes in him shall not perish but have everlasting life." It was on the side of a wee Gospel Hall church, I passed this place so many times before and paid no heed that it only then really hit me as to what this was and I went back to my flat repeating this scripture. This was the last time that I would stay in Whitburn as I had made up my mind to leave and a few days after this I remember one morning when I was laid out in my flat in withdrawal I had what I can only describe as an unexplainable few moments, the words 'Edinburgh' came into my head a few times and after this I was able to get up and walk out of the flat. I walked seven miles to Livingston to the hostel where I had lived when I was 16yrs old and was surprised that there was a worker who remembered me. He spoke to me and advised me to go to a place called Bethany House in Edinburgh. This was more evidence that I needed to go there as this was the third time that I had heard this that day. The worker gave me some food, £10 to get the train and directions to the hostel. I however got to the bus depot and bought a bus ticket instead as this was cheaper. I then bought some cider as I was desperate for a drink and drank this on the bus into Edinburgh. I got to the hostel sometime in the early evening and spoke to a worker there who let me know that there were no beds available. He gave me the address of a night shelter a few streets away that would take me in for the next few nights until a place became free in the Bethany hostel. The night shelter was a real eye opener. I remember when I woke up sober in the mornings realising where I was and feeling intimidated. There were over one hundred rooms which were smaller than a prison cell and these were occupied by some of the most hardened street homeless people I had ever met. I wondered how I'd ended up here. Each day I would walk back round to Bethany's door to be told that the bed was still not available.

I don't remember the exact date but I do remember the feeling of relief when I could finally move into the hostel. First, though I needed to have an induction. This was the first time I had been allowed into the Bethany building and I was greeted by a worker who then helped me with the paperwork to move in. It was then that I discovered this was a Christian hostel and that the workers were all born again Christians. They were working there to support others and to share their faith.

I had no idea what this meant as I had never been in a church other than to go to weddings or funerals. When I was taken into my room I remember being lost for words as even though it was small there was everything I needed; a bed including bedding, curtains and a lamp, and furniture. I had stepped from chaos into some sort of order. Everything was tidy and in its place and this completely took me by surprise. I had come from a chaotic lifestyle and was now confronted with order! This day marked the start of a beautiful transformation from a no-hoper to a man filled with joy. Bethany House was a gift sent by God.

Bethany House was started in the early 1980s by a church minister in Leith, Edinburgh to help with the ever-increasing homeless issue. He felt called to action by the Lord after countless homeless people were found sleeping at his church door. I met with this man several times and I was completely moved by his testimony and his faith to this God whom he served. In fact, every worker I met at Bethany at this time had this in common. They were completely devoted to this God and their passion for sharing Jesus was infectious. I continued to drink and use drugs at this time but I was starting to take an interest in this gospel truth and I went along to a few of the meetings to see what all the fuss was about. I spoke at length to many of the workers who would share their testimony of how they had been saved from their sins and how their lives had been changed. Some of the workers even had similar backgrounds to me. This gripped me further as I saw so much of myself in the stories that they were sharing. The hostel cook in particular would speak to me at every opportunity about his faith, sharing how he had been changed by God from a street drinker to being saved from his sin. There he was, now serving others in full time employment! I was intrigued by his passion and also quite scared of him at the same time as he recounted his wild days.

I spent the next few months in this hostel living the same life that I had lived up to that point using both drugs and alcohol and getting into trouble, but I sensed that something was changing within me as I had started to read the Bible. A copy had been left in the bedroom for me and when I read it, I would speak with the cook who would explain any questions that I had. I also attended the daily devotion meetings which were held in the hostel every afternoon just after lunch. During this time someone would read from the Bible and then they would explain it afterwards. I was listening and yet after these meetings I would go out and drink alcohol. I was still gripped by its power.

An older lady who used to do a night shift once a week at the hostel started to ask me if I would like to attend her church evening services on a Sunday. At the start I politely refused but I agreed one time and went along to see what it was like. I remember going in and feeling so out of place, the anxiety rising up within me. I looked down at the ground for most of the service to avoid eye contact as I didn't want anyone to speak with me or ask why I was there. I spent most of the service wishing that all the ladies would close up their handbags as I couldn't help looking at all the purses that I could steal. Thankfully I resisted and soon I started to go to this church every Sunday evening. When I would return I would pretend to the other residents that I had been somewhere else other than church to avoid any awkward questions.

CHAPTER 10

I continued to speak with the hostel cook almost every day and he would always ask if I was ready to invite the Lord Jesus into my heart. To be honest these questions he was asking really freaked me out and would always play on my mind later on into the evening until we would catch up the next day. This went on for another few weeks until I yelled at him, 'right what do I do as you are annoying the life out of me!' He laughed and then sat me down and explained that it was as simple as admitting that I was a sinner and saying sorry for all the bad things I had done and will do. Recognising my sin and repenting (turning around) of this and laying my life down at the feet of Jesus and living for Him. I remember saying 'Oh is that it?!' and again we both laughed. I told him I was ready and wanted to give my life to Jesus. At that point he invited another guy to come in to the kitchen and join us as we prayed this prayer, 'Lord Jesus, I am sorry for all the bad things that I have done and will do and recognise that I am a sinner and that I can't live this life on my own. I believe that you are the Son of God and that you died and you rose again. Come into my heart and be my Saviour, Amen. (If you have said this prayer even now as you read this and you want to know more then please link in with a local church.)

I would love to report that I was completely transformed but that was so far from the truth, in fact I
went out that evening to a bar in Edinburgh and drank
again. This would be the common trend for the next few
months but I do remember one significant change and
that was that I started to feel guilty after each drink and
after every bad thing that I did. I now know that this
was the power of Jesus starting to work in me. I would
talk to people when I was out in bars and tell them that
I was now a Christian. They laughed at me and thought
I was a madman, but even then it was clear that God
was working. I continued to meet with my keyworker
at the hostel and we discussed my recent conversion. He
knew that I had severe issues with substance abuse and
he suggested that I go and check out their Rehab unit
which was a short distance away. When I later met with
the manager my mind was made up and I asked to move
in. It would not be long after this that I made the short
journey to Bethany Christian Centre in Leith and unknown to me I was about to embark on the next step of
my walk. The centre was a beacon of hope for so many
people and I have the fondest memories of my time
there. I spent two stays there as I would relapse once,
but I remember meeting so many great guys who influ-
enced me and who I still have the upmost respect for.

The group of residents were a mixed bunch! From
hardened criminals and lifelong heroin addicts to street
drinkers who had become born again Christians! People
who were now on fire for Jesus Christ and had turned

their lives around to serve others. Our daily routine involved an 8am diary meeting, group sessions and volunteering in the afternoon, before we would settle down for the evening and eventually go to bed around 11.30pm. This was the structure my life was missing up until this point. Bethany offered me a haven away from addiction and the tools to put this in place. We would eat meals together as a family, we would have 'sharing meetings' in the evenings where we were encouraged to open up about how we were feeling. We would spend a lot of time chatting and being honest with each other and I have to admit that I was extremely dubious of this at the beginning. I spent a lot of the time not sharing how I was feeling for fear that I would be rejected again.

There is a serious dark side to addiction that people do not see, a side which robs people of their own lives and the lives of their friends and families. I look at my own addiction and the way that it made me so selfish to the point that I had lost all sense of morality where I did not care what I did or who I hurt. I remember when I was in the grip of addiction I would turn up at my mum's door in the middle of the night shouting to get her attention outside her house and causing so much of a scene so that she would give me money or food so that I would leave quickly. I remember also my little brother would look from the window eager to see his big brother but he would be ushered inside as they knew that I had no intention of seeing him at this point. I would only hurt him through my selfishness. My time in recovery allowed me to look honestly at my behaviour and to approach my thinking in a new way. We were encouraged to avoid 'stinking thinking' where we would look back at our old lives in a glorifying way.

CHAPTER 11

Bethany Christian centre was in the middle of Leith and surrounded by chaos. There were drug dealers living nearby and Leith walk was full of pubs and clubs. There was temptation everywhere but the one thing that Bethany had was the protection of the Holy Spirit. This allowed the residents who lived there ultimate protection if they took their recovery serious enough. When I allowed the Holy Spirit to work within me, He introduced me to new people who would have a major impact on my life. This included Dave who would teach me a few chords which led to me developing a desire to lead worship whenever I can. Paul and Alasdair were guys who showed me Jesus in every ounce of their beings and who could forget Eddie and Harry who showed me that even though we were saved, Christians could still have a bit of fun! We certainly did that! These guys have no idea the impact that they have had in my life, but I wanted to share this as without the support that I received from them I would not be here and would not be the man I am today.

I stayed in the rehab in recovery for the next ten months and I remember being in the centre for the millennium party (Year 2000) and I recall being really on edge as I wanted to leave so many times to go to the massive New

Year's Eve (Hogmanay) street party on Princes Street in Edinburgh. There were estimated to be a few hundred thousand people there and it was to be the party of the century. I remember sitting on the steps of the hallway in the centre facing the front door and contemplating leaving so many times. I spoke with a few of the workers again who reminded me that there was a party at the church across from the centre and that there would be some worship and then a ceilidh (Scottish traditional dance). This would bring in the new year celebrations and all the volunteers and workers along with residents would be there and we would all celebrate together. I'm glad that I listened to this advice as I enjoyed myself so much and this was drug free enjoyment! I have to admit it was the best fun I ever had! During this time I met a few people from Northern Ireland who were over visiting their sister who was volunteering in the centre. Unknown to me, these guys would become my family and the girl would end up being my wife and the mother of my 4 amazing children! Writing this now, I'm still blown away by the faithfulness of God!

The centre brought in so many volunteers every year from all over the world and I met many wonderful and diverse people. The girl I mentioned above was called Gillian and she lived in Fermanagh, Northern Ireland. She had taken a year out from a law degree and had decided to come to Edinburgh to work with vulnerable people. I remember when I met her for the first time I thought that she was very pretty however I was very serious about my recovery and I did not want to sway from this. I convinced myself that there would be no way that I would stand a chance with her as I still assumed that I was a worthless nobody who no one would love.

CHAPTER 12

I started to volunteer at a few different places over the city of Edinburgh over the next few months and did some removal work moving furniture for the Bethany shops. I then secured a spot doing some work at the city mission giving out soup and clothes to the street homeless who would call in for some food. I then got put in contact with a drugs education agency called 'Fast Forward' who offered free advice to schools and youth groups about drugs. I figured that this was the place for me and I spent the next while going around helping out there. I also at this time was conscious that I had never finished school so I headed to college with a good friend of mine 'Mikey'. We enrolled in a photography course (quickly changed this though as we had no cameras) and then we changed the course to do social care and health care. I had no idea that this would be the ideal course to do the job that I still do today. I completed levels 2 and 3 including a placement at a brain injury unit in Edinburgh. This was such an eye opener and I learnt so much from the wonderful people there.

My walk with Jesus was becoming more real as I was linked in with a local church and involving myself more in the devotional times at the centre. I was also spending a lot of time reading the Bible that I had been gifted by my keyworker. At this point I was given an opportunity to move into a halfway house which had been piloted as a discipleship house and where residents could move onto for a 6 month intensive Bible study. I grabbed this opportunity with both hands and at the tail end of summer 2000 myself and three other guys started on our journey through group sessions using three books: how to live like Jesus, how to serve like Jesus and how to minister like Jesus. This would turn out to be one of the most important steps that I took as it allowed me time to rest in the presence of God and to learn more about Him. My time in this house was amazing and I learnt so much about myself that I felt comfortable for the first time letting other people know about my faith in Jesus. It was in this house at 48 Kirk Street in Leith that I would have real encounters with God and really heard His voice for the first time.

We were in a Bible study one morning and were learning about the baptism of the Holy Spirit and I was extremely confused as I had no clue as to what this meant. When I queried this I was still no further forward in my quest for understanding and I uttered the words 'how can I understand this when I have never even been baptised?' As soon as I had said these words I heard the Lord say 'let's do this, get baptised! let's do this now, look there is water here' I dropped the books and said this to the group that I could not carry on with the study until I was baptised and that it needed to happen now. As soon as I mentioned this one of the other guys told me about Philip and the Ethiopian and explained that when Philip met this guy reading the scriptures he asked if he knew what they meant. The Ethiopian said he did and that he needed to be baptised immediately and that there was water right beside him so there was no need to wait. This was all the evidence that I needed that this was a command from the Lord and that I would be disobeying Him if I ignored this. We met with the managers and staff at Bethany and explained all this and at first we were met with opposition but I was adamant that I would be baptised that day and at approx. 3pm that day we had arranged a baptism service that would take place in the discipleship house with about thirty or so people praising the Lord with guitars and singing! What blessed memories those are!

On another occasion in the discipleship house I heard the voice of God when I was asleep. We had been discussing grief, dealing with past hurts and crying. I had shared that day that I hadn't cried in years and in fact I did not know how to do this now as I had built up a defence wall that nothing would faze me. God broke this wall down in a dream one night, I was asleep and had a vivid dream where I was crying out for help and no one would come to my assistance. I cried out 'God help me' and when I did this I heard a voice clearly saying, 'Why does it take something to happen for you to come to me on your knees in surrender?' As soon as this happened I awoke and the tears were rolling down my face and I cried for the next few days. This would be the start of an incredible journey of restoration where I would eventually deal with the past hurts that had stopped me moving forward in my walk with God. I would then meet again with my counsellor at the rehab centre to go through anger management and give over the issues that I had with my father and his abusive behaviour that I had never been able to deal with until this point. A year or so after this I would then arrive at my father's front door and knocking on the door would spend an afternoon with him telling him all about my faith. When I spoke with him, he apologised for his past behaviours. What a break-through! I could never have forgiven my father without the love of Christ.

The six month stay at the discipleship house flew by in a flash and I enjoyed this so much. I grew in my faith with the help of the other residents and the speakers who would give of their time to come in each day to take Bible studies and discussion times. When the time in the house was drawing to an end we all had decisions to make about what we would do next. We had discussed mission work and myself and another of the residents were really passionate about going off somewhere far and exotic in the hope of giving something back. We had a discussion with a minister who was leading one of our studies and he simply said, 'there is a mission field out your front door and sometimes you don't need to travel that far!' It soon became clear as to what God wanted me to do. After a conversation with the manager at the Rehab centre I applied for a volunteer post. I was interviewed and subsequently offered a placement at the very place I had been a resident several times before.

CHAPTER 13

I was buzzing to get started as I wanted to help others who were affected by addiction as I was. I had come full circle from resident to now working with guys like me. I absolutely loved working in the centre and have to say it did not feel like I was working at all. The centre is a beacon of hope in a city of darkness and is such a safe haven for people who have been ravished by addiction and hurt. Jesus' love flows through that place and I have so many great memories of praying with hurting people, praising Jesus in the quiet room to leading meetings upstairs. Many late nights were spent chatting in the quiet room to the small hours of the morning encouraging and introducing Jesus to lives who were in desperate need of a touch from the King of Kings.

It took me some time to find a church and I reckon I was trying to find the ideal church. A friend once told me that if I found the perfect church I would make it imperfect! I went to different churches weekly until I found AbbeyHill Baptist, a church at the top of Easter Road in Edinburgh where I settled and soon got involved playing guitar and then leading worship. I loved this church and learnt so much from the pastor there at that time.

Earlier I mentioned Gillian who was volunteering in the

centre. I saw her love for the Lord and how she was so confident working in the environment that she had been plunged into. By the end of her time there I had no doubt that I was falling for her. I attempted a few times to speak with her but never got the chance to say how I felt. On her last day they held a BBQ / praise night at the beach and there were loads of people there and I even attempted that night to chat with her but again things got in the way! It was looking more and more like she would return home and that I would have to wonder as to what could have been, but God had other plans as He always does and it would be a short time later that I would be on a plane for the first time in my life nipping over the Irish sea to land in Belfast to visit Gillian!

My first time on a plane, I am not afraid to admit, was a scary experience for me! Thankfully the flight was short (approximately 25mins), in fact it took longer checking in and out! The fear I felt on the flight was quickly replaced with excitement as I spent the most wonderful weekend with my soulmate. We went out for food, walks and best of all decided that we would start dating. This was the start of a two-year, long-distance relationship where we would see each other every two or three weeks and speak almost every night on the phone.

The first time I visited Gillian's family home in County Fermanagh will never leave my mind as I remember being so nervous about meeting them. We arrived on a Saturday and stayed a night and I immediately felt at home. It was so far removed from anything that I had ever experienced, for example her family would all eat around the table in the kitchen and discuss how everyone's week had been. This was totally alien to me and I remember feeling really upset on the trip back to Belfast as I realised what I had missed out on with my own family. I knew at this point that I wanted to spend the rest of my life surrounded by loving family and being an integral part of this. Whenever I would return back to Scotland, I always felt like I had left an important piece of me back in Northern Ireland. I would eventually find out that this was my heart and that I needed to move there.

Working in the Rehab centre allowed me to grow in my Christian faith and the more I served others the more I realised the potential within people. I quickly got to grips with being a worker as opposed to a resident. I completely immersed myself in this work and absolutely adored it so much so that I knew then that I needed to continue to work in this area. I continued with my studies at college whilst working at Bethany and gained qualifications in Social and Health care. The two years spent at Bethany flew past and I saw God's hand in so much of the work there. He gave me the privilege of leading hurting people to Jesus and mentoring guys who wanted to pack it all in and return to their ruined lives. Serving the men that came through those doors was so rewarding. We sang songs, prayed, cried with people and fed them through the never changing Word of God. Every day was different but the message was always the same - that the gift of the amazing grace of Jesus is available to all! There is a part of me that yearns to be back in Casselbank street in Leith with the most wonderful people that you would ever meet, but this can't be as there is a season for everything. Leaving the comfort and safety of Bethany was really hard to do but I was confident that I was going in the shelter of the Almighty who would guide me into a new chapter of my life.

CHAPTER 14

Gillian and I began discussing the future and praying about where God would lead us next. One Sunday night when I was visiting Belfast we went along to Fisherwick Presbyterian and I have to admit I really enjoyed the service. This church is situated in the student area of Belfast and at the evening services they have a high volume of students coming in and out. The lights were dimmed and the music was turned up loud! There were so many talented musicians that they were able to have two full bands leading the praise to Jesus. I felt a real sense of the Lord's presence and immediately felt at home.

During the announcements the minister brought up the subject of internship and that the programme was due to start again in September of that year. I couldn't get away from this thought and so I spoke with him afterwards and shared that I felt the Lord may be directing me to this role. We had a great conversation in which we agreed that I should go and pray about this and when I returned again in a fortnight we should meet and chat things through.

When I returned we had a lengthy conversation but this time we agreed that I should go for it. The minister had already started to spread the word of the new interns arriving and that there were a few from Northern Ireland, England, Hungary and one older guy from Scotland who would need accommodation for the duration of the internship (me!). He sourced a room for me in a house in the south of the city with a group of students. I remember visiting the house and meeting all the housemates who had clearly known each other for years and just feeling a real sense of community. I must have made an impression as all agreed that I should move in. This was answer to prayer and I remember thinking the Lord has a great sense of humour as I moved in with a student lawyer, two accountants and a guy doing a PHD in haematology! Not your usual ex-addict's social circle! However, I settled into life in Belfast very quickly. I packed up most of my belongings from the volunteer flat in Edinburgh and boarded the ferry to move onto a new life in Northern Ireland in 2003. Just before I left though, I had one last thing to do. This had been on my heart for a while; I needed to make things right with my dad. For years I had been harbouring hatred towards him for how he had abused and mistreated my mother, and also for him not being there for us as children. I felt I needed to address this before moving on.

I drove out to dad's house one evening with the plan that I would go to his door and see if he was sober enough to talk with. I was ready for anything, for an argument or even a fight, however when I arrived at his door he greeted me with warmth and invited me in. He introduced me to his new wife and my step sister. I was taken aback and not ready for this, however when I asked him to chat he invited me out the back and I took this to mean that he wanted to fight. I aggressively said, "let's go!"

We went outside and before I could utter a word he apologised for all the years that we had missed together and for the hurt he may have caused. Without a pause in breath I retorted that he was saying sorry to the wrong person and that he should have been apologising to my mother. He simply said that he couldn't. To this day I'm unsure if this was down to pride or shame. We carried on chatting for another few hours; I let him know that I was leaving to live in Northern Ireland and that I had surrendered my life to Jesus. I also told him that I had forgiven him and that I was sorry for any hurt that I had caused. This short time that I had with my dad was so precious as I was able to leave the hurt and pain that I had stored up for so long at the feet of Jesus and allow the Holy Spirit to change me from within. I felt so free after this, like a weight had been lifted from me. I hope that it affected him as much as it affected me.

CHAPTER 15

Soon after, I moved to Belfast and settled into a new life serving as an intern in Fisherwick Presbyterian church. I was blessed beyond belief and I was able to spend a lot more time with my soulmate Gillian. Belfast was certainly a different city to Edinburgh; it was five years since the Good Friday agreement and tension could still be felt at that time. There was the odd occasion when we would be evacuated from restaurants or shopping centres, but this soon settled and I quickly grew to love this new city. The work at the church was fantastic also and I absolutely loved the people whom I was working with. We served the older people in the church, the youth and all in-between and even set up student lunches every Thursday for the university students nearby. This was a great way to get to know the students and allow them time to share any worries or concerns they were experiencing. We even had the opportunity to pray with them.

I was given the opportunity to lead one of the groups of musicians in the church. We led the praise every fortnight and during this time the Lord allowed me to develop in the area of worship leading. I even started to write my own songs in the hope that I would use these to glorify the Lord by what he had done and continues to do in my life. I served on the prayer ministry team too. We met before the service to pray and we prayed with people after the service. I saw the Lord bless so many people through these ministries.

Alongside my internship I worked in a local hostel for homeless people. Their backgrounds included addiction, mental health issues and other social exclusion issues. I started off working one or two shifts a week which eventually led to full time employment as a support worker when my internship ended. I continued to lead worship at Fisherwick for another few years and during this period we saw Jesus move in mighty ways! With assistance from the church I was able to set up a small concept called 'Embrace on the streets' which was an idea I had in 2004. We saw an increase in foreign nationals arriving at the hostel with no jobs or money. This meant that they found themselves street homeless and without any financial support. My idea was a simple one; the local churches would come together to meet the basic needs of these people. I met with the local churches and drew up a list of items that we would need to collect, as well as a location to serve as a base. I had accessed similar support when I moved to Edinburgh and so this project was close to my heart. My hope was that even something small such as a change of clothes, would be the catalyst to a change in the way someone would approach life. I will never forget the ladies who clothed and fed me at the Cyrenians in Edinburgh all those years ago.

I'm sure you're wondering how the romance was going

at this stage! Well I was amazed at the way God took my broken life and set me completely free! He showered me with good things, with blessings and turned around even the hardest of hearts! He took a no hoper and filled him with JOY! Gillian and I dated for six years, got engaged in 2006 and then married in 2007. We married in Gillian's home church in the company of family and friends both old and new! This made me the happiest man on earth as I now had been blessed with a wife and a home just outside Castlederg in Northern Ireland. You can never know the complexity of being homeless until you are put in that position. Being blessed with a house felt like I was the king of my castle and I now knew that I had completely moved on from the past.

Travelling to Belfast to work in the hostel was not viable any more but God blessed me with a job in the same organisation in Londonderry. The team I work with in Derry are fantastic support workers as they seek to provide the best service to the people we meet. It's not an easy job as we often encounter aggression and challenging incidents, but I'm so thankful to God for the opportunities that He continually leads me into.

As we had set up home in Castlederg, we attended Gillian's home church; a small country Church of Ireland parish with a lot of members belonging to it from the local area. We went along each Sunday morning for the next few years and volunteered in the youth work that the church ran. Although we met lovely people we felt that God was directing us to find a church much closer to home. As we visited some of the local churches, we met some wonderful people who have left a lasting impact on our lives; real people with real issues who we never heard complain! They chose to live out their Christian faith in the way that the Bible tells us to – relying daily on God for strength and help.

At this time I took an interest again in song writing and sharing my testimony in different places. I also met some great friends who are still in my life to this day; friends I can call upon to pray or just to chat with and to offload should I have things that are burdening me. It was through one of these prayer times with friends that we began to pray for a non-denominational church to come to Castlederg. God answered this need and we started to attend Castlederg Christian Fellowship in the Autumn of 2017. We have been blessed to be a part of this new venture and have seen the Lord's hand in all that is done in this church. It is located in the science room of the Pastor's old high school where his teachers would teach that God does not exist! How amazing that he is now in the same room preaching the gospel of the risen Jesus Christ! We have witnessed a pouring out of blessing in the Castlederg area as a result of this work being set up.

CHAPTER 16

Gillian and I had always planned on starting a family and we were blessed with our first born, Sophie, in April 2010. I was simply blown away with emotion when she was born; I was a blubbering wreck! When she arrived home from the hospital she responded well to music and I attributed this to me playing guitar and singing to her when Gillian was pregnant. Sophie has grown into the most wonderful child who loves people and loves singing and drama! Harry was born in April 2012 and we were completely overcome with joy when he was born. I was super excited that he would carry on the Goldie name! Harry took a while settling in the evening and could be heard every night from 5pm until about 7pm screaming from the top of his lungs. This is a useful skill for him now when he's on the football pitch! Sam was born in......you guessed it! April 2014 and we quickly learnt that he was not going to let his big brother and sister boss him around. Sam loves being first for everything, even if that is something trivial like lining up at the front door of the house to get into the car! I love singing with my children and have done so since they were babies. We regularly have praise times in the house, read Scripture and pray as these are valuable life experiences that I missed out on as a child. Sophie, Harry and Sam all profess to have a faith in Jesus and have surrendered their lives to Him. This is only the beginning for them and it is mine and Gillian's job to teach them on a daily basis of the grace and the gospel of Jesus. It is our desire that they grow into mature Christians who are willing to make a stand for the gospel in this fallen world.

Gillian and I have been blessed with four wonderful children. God granted us another pregnancy in 2017 and after the 12 week stage things were going well so we shared our good news with family and friends. However, closer to the 20 week stage we were told that our baby boy was not growing to the normal size and that a weekly check-up was necessary to gauge how things were progressing. By week 25 we were dealt with the most devastating news that our son had 'Edwards Syndrome' and would most likely not make it to full term. Even if he did, he would die within hours of being born. We were heartbroken but we did not give up hope of a miracle. Teams of people prayed for healing but sadly this was not to be. Our beautiful boy Seth ('appointed by

God') was born sleeping at 28 weeks on the 3^{rd of} April in 2018.

Seth was beautiful and had the same small features as his siblings. His birth was surreal as there was no crying, just silence. He was measured and weighed as normal, dressed and then whisked away to have photographs taken by the empathy-filled midwives who made this traumatic experience more bearable. When we got to hold him it felt so heartbreakingly special. The hospital staff who cared for us were wonderful, from the nurses to the cleaners! I'd love to give special mention to Noreen who was the sister in charge of the ward and who spent that first day speaking with us and getting to know us. We were able to share our faith with her and we found out afterwards that many in the ward had been chatting about how our faith was carrying us through. We spoke of our love of the Lord Jesus and how He had set us free. Having this assurance and walking daily with God, we have everything we need.

I wrote a song for Gillian shortly after Seth's death and wrote it as if Seth was writing it to us.

Steadfast love fills my heart
A heart that never grew
I'm safe here in the arms of Jesus
His love is for me and you

Even though you are hurting
Please be filled with joy
I'm singing here with the angels
Your beautiful baby boy

The pain that you are feeling
The loss that you're going through
Please take heart and trust
That Jesus is enough for yourself

His love never ever fails
Jesus' love never runs dry
I'm safe here with the Saviour
So please do not cry
Sometimes everyone truly hurts

Please take heart
I'm waiting for you in Glory

The pain of losing a child is so immense that you simply can't write it down in words and it would be unfair to say that it only affects you; we and our extended family were deeply affected by this tragedy. Processing our loss was so difficult and at times we were angry that God had allowed this to happen. It felt like a part of us had been ripped away. Why hadn't God answered our prayers? If He is the God of miracles, why hadn't He performed one for us? This shook us to the core but we are so thankful to have our faith in God, whose ways are much higher and greater than ours. Even though we don't understand this test, we know that Seth is waiting for us in Glory and that one day we will be reunited with our precious boy. What a day that will be! We speak about him most days with the children and if we don't mention him they will quickly correct us by including their little brother too. This blesses my heart!

CLOSING REFLECTION....

CHAPTER 17

I love the ultimate freedom that I have received by simply trusting Jesus and allowing Him into my life. He has transformed me and I'm so grateful for the countless times that the Lord has blessed me beyond belief. I look at the gift of prayer that He freely gives us and recognise that is a continued channel to Him. I'm so grateful for the Holy Spirit who works in us and through us. God has the power to change the hearts of everyone without HOPE and to fill them with JOY! I thank God that the person I have become today can empathise with people struggling with the same issues. I can tell them that Jesus has the power to transform the hardest of hearts and I am testimony of this. I had no church upbringing and absolutely no interest in the gospel but God rescued me from this mindset and showed me the true meaning of life is in Jesus. The reason we are here is to worship the Creator! Jesus is the way, the truth and the life, all of creation needs to bow down and confess that He is Lord!

Over the past few years, we have been experiencing unprecedented times, a global pandemic, war, humanitarian and financial crises. The one thing that remains unchanged however is the unconditional love of God. That same love sent His son Jesus to walk the road to Calvary, carry His own cross and bear our punishment for us. He is the same yesterday, today and forever! His love never fails and never runs dry! Go and tell this broken, hurting world that they need a Saviour! Repent, turn to him, confess that we are full of sin and allow Him to work in us and through us for His Glory.

Sin is real
Jesus is real
Repentance is free
Turn to the Saviour!

A COLLECTION OF SOME OF MY POETRY / SONGS……..

TO WALK WITH GOD

The world's aim is to confuse
To keep you in it's strife
Have you heard the good news
Jesus speaks into your life

He's calling us to holiness
Out of complete emptiness
Replaces our utter loneliness
The Lord in his faithfulness

To walk with the Lord
Submit to his ways
Trust in his holy word
Offer him our praise

He calls us to turn around
From the sin that would bind
All our sin on him was found
So new life we will find

As Jesus walked, so should we
Trust and follow him now
Sets us free how can it be
Our sin stains on his brow

I TRUST JESUS

I trust Jesus
Nothing else will do
I trust Jesus
His sacrifice was for me and you

I trust Jesus
Fills us full of hope
I trust Jesus
When we can not cope

I trust Jesus
His heart is pure love
I trust Jesus
He intercedes from above

I trust Jesus
When the world is against me
I trust Jesus
His love has set me free

I trust Jesus
His heart is to know you
I trust Jesus
His mercy carries you through

I trust Jesus
Submitting to your grace
I trust Jesus
I long to see your face

I trust Jesus
The Holy spirit leads us
I trust Jesus
His grace truly frees us

WHEN I FALL

When the world holds its grip around me
And I feel I can't let go
Of the thoughts and fears that surround me
And make me lose control

You heal me with your power
Restore the strength within
I trust in your amazing grace
And lay my life down at your feet

For you my God are faithful
You never fail
You are the way
The truth and the life

And through it all
You catch me when I fall
I put my trust
In the one who gave it all

HOPE IS FOUND
AT THE CROSS

Hope is found at the cross
Healing found in the blood
Freedom found at the feet of Jesus
Hope is found at the cross

Jesus
Giver of life
Jesus
Arms open wide
Jesus
Took my guilt
Jesus
Set me free

I TURN TO YOU

Before I met you I carried it all
The weight of the world and it's trials
Suffering anguish, pain and strife
You called my name

The name above names calling mine
Crying for me in my sin
Bore from me through
Through the death on a cross

I turn to you
Looking to you
Cast my cares
Leave them behind

Jesus take my life
Make it new
Set me free
To live for you

TEARS

Through trials and tribulation
When you feel like you're going insane
All the world is against you
And you feel nothing but pain

I know you are by my side
I know you never hide
When I feel fear you are there
Because you care

You in me, I in you
You're with me whatever I go through
Through all my fears and all my pain
When the world just drives me insane

You will wipe away my tears

THERE IS A WAY

There is a way
A way to father
Where death is beaten
Curse is lifted away

Our eyes are open
Tears wiped away
Weary are built up
Blessed beyond the curse

From no hope to full of joy
We are given new life
A touch from the king that heals the broken
Breaks the chain, sets captives free

A blessing for all
All who believe

GRACE

The cross has power
His blood sets us free
Restoring the broken
Thank you for saving me

Through Jesus we have life
The good news of the Lord
Broken lives are made new
By the power of his word

A gift so undeserved
We can't earn his grace
Simply to the cross we cling
Looking to his glorious face

Gods grace never fails
His mercy never leaves
Salvation is a free gift
To everyone who believes

THANKS.......

I want to take a moment to acknowledge some people who without their love and support I would not have got to the point whereby I have penned my book, special thanks to Glenda for editing and making sense of my words and producing such a wonderful piece of literature. Thank you to my wife Gillian for all the support that you give, few people possess the considerate, unselfish, loving heart that you have, I thank you for being the amazing person that you are, I am blessed to have you in my life. I want to thank my children whom I love dearly, you give me so much joy. Thanks to Alasdair for believing and giving me the tools needed to overcome and showing me Jesus, Thanks to Dave, Paul, Eddie and Harry and to all the guys at the centre whom I love dearly. Thank you to all my friends old and new who give so much support.

I want to thank my Lord and saviour Jesus who bore my sins on calvary, set me free, saved me from certain death, how can I not praise your name. you took a no hoper and filled him with joy. Thank you Jesus

EPILOGUE

I struggled with fear and worry for years. But through time, I began to find that the things that once would have sent me down an anxious spiral, no longer had the same effect. It didn't happen quickly, but over days, months, years.

I read words - of life - of truth - his truth. Soaking them in, praying them out loud. Until they became so familiar, they replaced the other things in my mind that I'd battled against. There's power in God's word. Change happened. Anxious thoughts began to diminish. Worry let go of its constant grip. And though fear is sometimes still there, it no longer wields any control, holding me back, paralyzing me in its grasp.

It's not always easy, and it often comes down to a choice:

Choose to not allow fear and anxiety to control your life.
Choose to guard your heart.
Choose to surrender your life to the Lord Jesus.
Choose to focus your mind on what is true in the midst of uncertain times

We might still feel afraid, but we can believe that God is with us. We may not be in control, but we can trust the One who is. We may not know the future, but we can know the God who does. Thank you Jesus.

"For God has not given us a spirit of fear, but of power and of love and of a sound mind." ~ 2 Timothy 1:7

Printed in Great Britain
by Amazon

40499758R00046